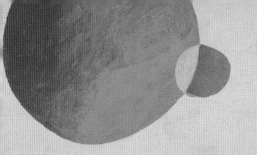

A poem by

LANGSTON HUGHES

Lullaby

(For a Black Mother)

Illustrated by

SEAN QUALLS

HARCOURT CHILDREN'S BOOKS
Houghton Mifflin Harcourt
Boston   New York   2013

"Lullaby (For a Black Mother)" from *The Collected Poems of Langston Hughes* by Langston Hughes, edited by Arnold Rampersad
with David Roessel, associate editor, copyright © 1994 by the Estate of Langston Hughes
Reprinted by arrangement with Alfred A. Knopf, a division of Random House, Inc.
Illustrations copyright © 2013 by Sean Qualls
"A Note about the Poet" text copyright © 2013 by Pink Moon Studio

The photograph of Langston Hughes and his mother is reprinted by permission of Harold Ober Associates Incorporated and is from the
Yale Collection of American Literature, Beinecke Rare Book and Manuscript Library.

Harcourt Children's Books is an imprint of Houghton Mifflin Harcourt Publishing Company.
www.hmhbooks.com

The text in this book was set in Aros and Adobe Garamond.
The display type was set in Aros.
The illustrations were done in acrylic, pencil, and collage.

Library of Congress Cataloging-in-Publication Data
Hughes, Langston, 1902–1967.
Lullaby (for a Black mother) / Langston Hughes ; illustrated by Sean Qualls.
p. cm.
Includes bibliographical references (p. 28).
ISBN 978-0-547-36265-6
1. Infants—Juvenile poetry. 2. Mother and child—Juvenile poetry. 3. Lullabies, English—United States.
4. African Americans—Juvenile poetry. 5. Children's poetry, American. I. Qualls, Sean, ill. II. Title.
PS3515.U274L85 2012
811'.54-dc22
2012025484

Manufactured in China
SCP 10 9 8 7 6 5 4 3 2 1
4500391167

For my wife, Selina—
mother of my children,
muse of my art—S.Q.

My little dark baby,
My little earth-thing,
My little love-one,

What shall I sing
For your lullaby?

Stars,
Stars,
A necklace of stars

Winding the night.

My little black baby,
My dark body's baby,
What shall I sing
For your lullaby?

Moon,
Moon,
Great diamond moon,

Kissing the night.

Oh, little dark baby,
Night black baby,

Stars, stars,
Moon,
Night stars,
Moon,

For your sleep-song lullaby!

A Note about the Poet

Langston Hughes with his mother in 1902

It's nighttime in Harlem, and beneath a blanket of stars a young man sits down and writes a poem. He is alone. He has no kids of his own. For whom is he writing this lullaby?

James Mercer Langston Hughes was born just shy of midnight on February 1, 1902, in Joplin, Missouri. Not long after, his father left and moved to Mexico. His mother, working at one menial job after another, was often gone. As a boy, Langston was lonely. He lived with his stoic grandmother, who told him stories while wrapped in the bullet-riddled shawl that had belonged to her freedom-fighting husband.

Whenever his mother did come home, she and Langston would go to the library. Langston loved the way it smelled, its smooth wood tables, and especially its books. Books took Langston's blues away. They even gave him a dream: to become a poet.

Inspired by music—from hymns to jazz to blues— Langston wrote poems that were both plainspoken and lyrical. His poems express the richness, joys, and sorrows of everyday life and everyday people. He also wrote novels, plays, short stories, essays, autobiographies, libretti, and children's books.

The Dream Keeper and Other Poems, published in 1932, included "Lullaby (For a Black Mother)." In this collection, Langston wrote of the moon and the rain, rivers and fairies. He wrote of maple-sugar children in sugar houses and boys who carry "beauties in their hearts." He wrote of the night and stars. And he wrote of dreams. Langston was a dream keeper, and poems were his way to wrap dreams up in a soft blanket and keep them safe.

"Lullaby (For a Black Mother)" was written when Langston was a young man. Its sweet, lulling rhythm celebrates a bedtime ritual and the bond between a mother and child. Langston wrote poems for everyone. But perhaps he wrote this lullaby as a comfort to the lonely boy he had been.

Further Reading

The Collected Poems of Langston Hughes, edited by Arnold Rampersad, with David Roessel
The Dream Keeper and Other Poems by Langston Hughes, illustrated by Brian Pinkney
I, Too, Sing America: The Story of Langston Hughes by Martha E. Rhynes

Lullaby
(For a Black Mother)

My little dark baby,
My little earth-thing,
My little love-one,
What shall I sing
For your lullaby?
    Stars,
    Stars,
      A necklace of stars
      Winding the night.
My little black baby,
My dark body's baby,
What shall I sing
For your lullaby?
    Moon,
    Moon,
      Great diamond moon,
      Kissing the night.
Oh, little dark baby,
Night black baby,
    Stars, stars,
    Moon,
    Night stars,
    Moon,
For your sleep-song lullaby!